Baby Girl

Baby Girl Series #1

Rachel Angel

AUTHOR'S NOTE

Thank you for picking up Baby Girl, the first book in the Baby Girl Series.

This series is a New Adult Dark Bully Romance and contains bullying, sex, and some triggers. Recommended for 18+.

Summary

I thought he was just a figment of my imagination. The tall, dark, and handsome man who kept watch over me in the most beautiful garden I had ever dreamed of.

It wasn't just a garden, though, but a playground where he would teach me how to use my body and how to hone it into a secret human weapon. He said it would come in handy one day, and that I must master the art.

This man, who always wore a mask, said that learning the art of combat and defense would save my life. I just didn't know that it would require taking a life of someone I knew.

He called me *Baby Girl*, and after all of these years, I still quiver when I hear his name. My teacher, my lover. The ultimate bully. Now my Enemy.

**The Baby Girl Series is a Dark New Adult Romance with a TV-MA rating suited for 18 and up.

Prologue

<u>Calla</u>
Age 19
2 Years Ago
Casa Capri

The only thing I remembered was my name: Calla, which meant *Beauty* in Greek.

From the way he looked at me behind the black leather mask that covered the upper-half of his face with large cat-like slits for his aqua blue eyes, he seemed to agree with the meaning of it.

"You're awake," he said with a British accent. "About time."

"What do you mean?" I said, touching my head. Something was wrapped around it, and parts of my head felt numb. *"What is on my head?"* I asked, wanting to tear it off.

"Don't worry," the man said. "Even with bandages around your pretty head, you're still a knockout."

Knockout? Did I even cared about that? The least of my worries was how I looked. I couldn't even remember who I was, let alone how I looked. I glanced down. I thought I was in a bed since I had just woken up. My legs were covered with a soft cashmere-like blanket, but I could barely feel them. I tried to remember how I got here, but nothing came to me. Nothing at all, as though I didn't have any memories except for my name. *Calla.*

"And why am I sitting in this wheelchair?"

The man with the aqua blue eyes chuckled. His voice was melodic and smooth, with the vibrations and strength like a trained opera singer. His smooth tanned skin shone golden like a God, and he appeared ageless at first. But upon further inspection, he glowed with the vigor and strength of youth, around ten years older than me. Definitely more worldly, more experienced in life.

He smiled, making me notice his full lips, angular chin with a cleft in the middle, and straight white teeth. Despite the mask covering his face, he was a very handsome man. Beautiful even, as his high cheekbones, facial structure, and wavy black hair resembled those of the Greek statues that lined the large park-like garden surrounding us. Perhaps he was a Greek God statue come to life?

"Where are we?" I asked.

From the carefully-trimmed topiaries, statues, and an ancient fountain shaped like Neptune, I could guess we were at a five-star hotel in Rome or France.

The man simply said, "We are in the garden of my home."

I turned my head to try to see the "home" he gestured at behind me, but a sharp pain suddenly hit my neck, and I cried out.

"Easy now," the man said. "You haven't fully recovered."

"From what?" I asked.

"You don't remember?" he asked, looking at me curiously.

"No," I said. "I don't remember. If I did, why would I be asking?"

"The accident?" he asked examining my face with his steely blue eyes.

"What accident?" I asked.

Again his steely eyes regarded me carefully. His eyes darted to my lips and back to my eyes. "Do you remember anything?"

I tried to remember anything about myself, but came up with nothing. I shook my head. "Only that my name is Calla."

His full lips broke into a smile. "*Calla*. Such a beautiful name for a beautiful girl."

I smiled back, mesmerized by the strange sensations that heated up between us.

He reached out to touch my bottom lip with his thumb, which sent shocks of electricity through me. Rubbing my lip, I felt the area between my legs clench with a throbbing sensation. A hunger for more of his touch filled me, and an urge to moan shot through me. "Baby Girl," he called me. "For now, you may not remember anything except your name, but someday you will regain your memories. For now," he rubbed his thumb along the contour of my lower lip, before dipping it into my mouth, "you will be a guest of mine at *Casa Capri* for as long as you wish."

He continued rubbing my lip and dipping it into my mouth, until I could no longer hold back my moan. My mouth closed gently on his thumb and began sucking on him.

His brilliant blue eyes darted to my mouth as he bit the bottom lip of his, before closing his eyes. "You have such a sensual mouth, Bambina." He opened his eyes and sucked in a breath before removing his thumb. "You will find Casa Capri to be a place of rejuvenation and transformation. My sanctuary will become your sanctuary. In time, you will remember who you are, and I will help you."

I smiled, grateful to this kind, beautiful, and extremely sensual man who took pity on me… just a stranger who showed up at his home. The fact he wore a mask did not matter. It only added to his mystery and to my attraction to him. My body had already reacted hungrily towards him, eliciting sensations in me that made me feel so much…so so much, despite the fact I was sitting in a wheelchair.

He saw me looking down at my legs and said, "And I will help you mend your broken body. In time, you will be back to being yourself, but stronger." He smiled at me and then bent down to kiss me on my forehead.

I could not believe how fortunate I was to have landed on this man's doorstep. This beautiful, sexy, angelic man who already had me shivering when he called me *Baby Girl*, an endearment that sounded so possessive, sensual, and loving coming from his lips.

"Thank you," I said. "I don't know how to repay you for your kindness, uh…"

"You can call me *Gabriel*," the man said. He looked me over with a sweep of his eyes, taking me all in, including the bandages on my head. "And I can think of some way you can repay me," he smiled a slow sensual smile.

At that moment, I knew my stay at Casa Capri would not be a short one. By my own wish and desire, I wanted to know everything about this mysterious *Gabriel*. I wanted to be with him in every way.

I knew that Gabriel was going to be more than my host at Casa Capri. He was going to become my everything.

Chapter 1

<u>Calla</u>
Age 21
Present Day
London, England

The black of night, mixed with fog that had rolled in was the added layer that helped cloak me like a velvet blanket descended from the sky. As my heart was pounding, beating relentlessly against my chest, louder than the silence that surrounded me, I felt the stillness of the night echo like a rhythm. Any shifting of my well-trained body lying prone stomach down arms braced against the edge of the building's rooftop would break the silence. Any intake of a deep shaky breath which my body craved would shatter the rhythm of silence along the black-cloaked night.

Until someone opened the window from the top floor luxurious presidential suite of the Grand Olympia Hotel across from my building. The beat of the euro pop music streaming from the suite pounded faster than my heartbeat into the night, as glamorous rail-thin young women in slinky dresses and overly-made-up faces danced to the beat. I could see men with greasy grey hair, bloated faces, and wrinkly suits groping them.

"Disgusting motherfuckers," I whispered.

Peering through the high-powered scope of my precision long-range rifle, I trained my eyes toward my target, sweeping the room through the opulent window-heavy suite, built to offer the most spectacular view of the city of London and the River Thames from every room. To the left, the suite was filled wall-to-wall with people in various stages of undress, people snorting drugs, while others engaged in orgies.

Where the fuck was he?

Where was the host of this sleaze-fest?

I swept to the far right to what looked like a luxurious bedroom. There he was, the host himself, a grotesque-looking balding man in his late 50s, wearing only a thong and a silk red robe, his pot-bellied flab protruding over his thong. He was alone with a young woman, prettier than the others in his hotel suite…and younger. Also unlike the other girls in the suite, she wasn't high with a glassy gaze. Her eyes were terrified, clearly afraid of the man in front of her.

There you are, you gross fucker.

I steadied my aim at him, my finger ready to end the asshole, but my intentions were thwarted when he grabbed the girl, tore off her dress, and placed her in front of him, his chubby fingers groping her ass.

Damn, I can't take the shot.

Get out of the way, Girl! I wanted to shout to her.

As if she could hear me, she was turned around by the man to face the window. She had her arms up, trying to fight him off, but he had slapped her a few times before he bent her over, and began banging into her like an animal.

Shoot, get out of the way, Girl!

I tried to get a clear shot, but she was still in front of him.

Finally, in a split second he shoved her out of his way, and she ran out of the room, crying, I took my shot, straight into his balls.

I watched as his balls splatter in front of him, causing him to fall back onto the bed behind him.

That should have done the job.

But he got up, his hands holding his bloody crotch, screaming his head off in pain before he stared straight out the window to where I was, as though he could see me with some superhero sight, an assassin cloaked in the blackness of the night.

He was one tough motherfucker, that was sure, and the fact he was so high he could withstand the pain, like some zombie soldier made him a dangerous adversary.

When he made eye contact with me, and started shouting, yelling for *help*, I took another shot right when the door to his room opened.

Bullseye. The shot zipped through his forehead, and he collapsed. Dead.

I collapsed my rifle and packed it into a girly pink carry on, and ran toward the stairs to head down the building when a small army of muscled men with shaved heads rushed into the man's bedroom.

I ran down the stairs as fast as I could, donning my black jacket, my black cap, my black gloves, and pulling out the skirt of my dress out of my black leggings to create an elegant and sophisticated attire. I whipped off my ponytail holder to let my wavy brunette hair cascade down my shoulders and back, before slipping my feet from my sneakers into a pair of elegant but sensible heels.

I walked calmly across the street to stand in front of the hotel's door along with a few of the hotel's guests, and waved down a cab.

Just as the muscled men rushed out of the hotel's main entrance, a cab stopped in front of me, and I piled in, closing the door behind me.

"Where to, Miss?" the young attractive blonde man asked.

"You can drop me off on Bond Street," I said. "I'd like to do some shopping before I head out to the airport."

"End of your holiday?" the cab driver asked in a marvelous British accent. "American?" He looked me up and down, his eyes lingering on the valley between my breasts made more enticing by the deep plunge of my dress.

"I'm afraid I have to," I said. "Night flight so I can go to work right away when I land," I said. "Yes, American."

He smiled. I have an idea what he was thinking about. "That's too bad, love, I could have shown you a lot more of England, if you have time. A lot more."

"Yes," I said, smiling at him. "It is too bad. I really enjoyed my stay here, as short as it was."

"Well, if you ever come visit again and need a cab," he said, "Ring me or text me," he said, handing me a card.

I took it just as he stopped in front of Bond Street. "Thanks, Henry," I said, paying him for the ride.

"I can wait here while you shop and take you to the airport," he said.

"No," I said. "I'm meeting a friend, and he'll take me there."

Henry's smile faded and said, "Oh, a male friend. Well, if you change your mind, you have my card."

"Sure," I said, walking off, and very aware of his gaze on my rear end.

When I walked into the Arcade and disappeared from the cab's view, I walked quickly out the back, down another street and then a few more streets until I came into an area of high-end townhomes.

Walking up the steps to the entrance of one of them, I entered a key code to open the door to my home.

Chapter 2

<u>Calla</u>
Age 21
Present Day
London, England

"Nice place you have here, Calla," a smooth seductive masculine voice said from my bedroom.

My heart skipped a beat as my entire being recognized the owner of that mesmerizing sexy voice. I haven't heard that sound for almost half a year.

Yet every night, I could hear his voice in my head, in my thoughts, in my heart.

Gabriel. My Gabriel.

"Calla. Calla, my beautiful Bambina," Gabriel called out to me. "Come in here and let me see you as I love seeing you."

I dropped my bag before donning my dress and leggings as I walked seductively into my bedroom and was rewarded with the appreciative hungry look of the man who held my heart.

Gabriel was lying on my bed, his tanned muscular body contrasting against the all-white of my cream silk sheets. As my mind had pictured him many times, and as I have seen him many times, he was naked in his glorious muscular form and hard.

His hands were stroking his thick shaft, which was longer and harder than I had ever seen it.

"Missed me?" I asked huskily.

"Do you have to ask?" he said, his eyes devouring me from head to toe. "You've grown even more beautiful, Baby Girl." He got off the bed to walk towards me.

I waited with bated breath for him to reach me.

"Let me show you how much I missed you, Baby Girl," he said so low that it came out as a growl. He kissed me lightly on my lips and held me in his arms. "So tense, Baby Girl. Did you have any problems?"

I drew in a shaky breath and almost threw up. Gabriel gently stroked my back, easing my anxiety.

"I think I know what you need," he said hoarsely and reached down to my clitoris, gently stroking it until I was moaning with need and dripping wet. Gabriel smiled, as his fingers dipped into my wetness. "Yes, this is what you need right now," he said, rubbing my clit harder before he pinched it, sending me to open my mouth to gasp. Once open, his mouth clamped down on mine, devouring me with his tongue and lips before moving down to kiss my chest, my nipples, my stomach and the tip of my clit. "Ah, my Bambina," he said. "It's been too long since you've had my tongue on you. Much too long since you've had my cock drive into you." His mouth hover over my clit as his hot breath tickled my folds. "I want to eat you slowly savoring every delicious lick."

He got on his knees in front of me and placed his hands on each of my butt cheeks, pulling me tight to his mouth where he locked down, devouring me with light strokes that grew more and more passionate until I was bucking.

"Oh, Gabriel," I panted. "Take me now."

He tightened his grip on my buttocks and pulled me closer until I was on top of him, and he was eating me deep within. The sensations his mouth created in me was too much, and I rolled my head back, closing my eyes. "Fuck me now, Gabriel. Fuck me hard," I cried out.

With a groan, he tore his mouth from me, picked me up with one arm and swung me onto my bed. "How hard do you want me, *Bambina*?" he asked.

"So hard I can only see stars," I said.

"I'm going to give you what you need," he groaned, positioning himself at my entrance of my core. "You're so wet, I'm going to have to drive into you faster and deeper so you can feel every fucking stroke of my cock," he said, plunging deep into me so hard I flew up into the headboard of the bed.

"Yes!" I grunted. "Yes, that's it."

"Feel how much my cock wants you?" Gabriel grunted, driving into me again and again. "Feel every single stroke?"

"Yes, God yes!" I moaned.

"We were made for each other," Gabriel grunted, as he pumped deeply into me until sweat poured from his brow.

"Yes," I clawed at his back. "My body was made for you, Gabriel. Only you."

"Fucking right," he groaned. "Your body craves my cock like life. Look how you swallow up my cock, taking it deep into your very soul."

"Oh yes, Gabriel," my body can't live without yours. I need you so much!"

"Yes, Baby Girl," he grunted, turning me around and pulling me up on my knees to enter me from behind.

"Oh God," I moaned as he continued driving into me relentlessly. "I'm so…"

I shuddered, feeling the wave of sheer pleasure fill me.

"Come, Baby Girl," Gabriel coaxed. "Come hard for me!"

I exploded the moment he spanked me and roared his climax so loudly, the room shook.

I collapsed face down on the bed as he fell on top of me and rolled over to pull me into his arms. He kissed my temple. "I'm proud of you, Baby Girl. You did well on your first assignment. He was a very bad human being, and you did the world a favor tonight. He will no longer be terrorizing the people of small towns, killing innocent people, and kidnapping girls."

"I saw him with that missing girl," I said. "I wanted to get him before he raped her, but she was in front of him…"

"You did what you could do," Gabriel said. "Don't beat yourself up over it."

"I wished I could have gotten him sooner," I said.

"I know, Baby Girl. I wished we could have, too, since no one seemed to want to lay a hand on him."

"He's gotten away with so many years of crime," I said.

"And he would have kept getting away with it if you hadn't stopped him," Gabriel said, kissing my temple and holding me tightly. "My little *Bambina* was the only one brave enough to stop him."

"But you were the one who taught me everything," I said, kissing his cheek. "You found me on the shores of your island, took me into your house, took care of me, healed my injuries, and made me strong."

"You were always strong," Gabriel said.

"But you made me stronger," I said. "I owe you so much, Gabriel. I love you so much."

Gabriel kissed my lips then and said, "I love you too, Baby Girl. So much that it pains me."

Chapter 3

<u>Calla</u>
Age 19
2 Years Ago
Casa Capri

When Gabriel had found me on the shores of his island, my legs had been mangled, almost shredded by the jagged rocks along the shore. It took months for me to finally stand and walk without the need of a wheelchair. It would be several more months later where I could finally run.

I had never appreciated the fundamental ability to stand on my own two feet, to leap up into the air, and to even take a step forward.

"Baby Girl," Gabriel beamed at me. "You're walking! You're out of your chair and walking, my Miracle Girl!"

His smile was all the encouragement I needed to move my legs one step further and further towards him.

"Come to me," Gabriel beckon. "Come into my arms so I can hold and kiss you."

I took another step with my atrophied legs, one foot after another, as difficult as it was.

"You're stronger than you think, Baby Girl," Gabriel called out. "The strongest person I know. Now make up your mind and come to me."

Wincing in pain, I lifted my concrete legs placing one foot at a time in front of me, little by little, one step at a time. Until I was in his arms, crying large grateful tears, as Gabriel cried with me.

Gabriel wiped the tears from my cheeks and lightly touched my head. "Gone are your bandages from your head. Gone are your bruises. Now you're walking. Soon you will be running, jumping, and flying."

"Flying?" I asked.

"Yes, Baby Girl," Gabriel smiled. "I will teach you to fly…to glide, to land… out of airplanes, with hang gliders, jets, and whatever man can invent to take to the skies. You will soon be able to live as fully as you were meant to be."

"With you?" I asked. "I need you to be with me to do all this, Gabriel."

"I'll be there for you, Baby Girl," he said. "I will be there all the way."

"You'll help me avenge my family, won't you?" I asked. "That's why I'm here. I'm the lone survivor of a violent crime."

"Yes," Gabriel said, "my poor Baby Girl. I'll help you. I'll help you become the strong warrior woman that you are."

"Gabriel," I cried. "You're all I have. I love you. I love you. Take me. Make me yours."

I tried to kiss his lips. I tried to lean my body into his, to grind up against him, offering him my body.

Gabriel avoided my kiss, turning his face away. He pulled his body away from mine so my body wasn't grinding up against him. "I wished I could, but I'm not for you, Baby Girl. You should not be with me."

"But I love you, Gabriel. I want to be your woman." I tried to kiss him again. "Don't you find me beautiful? Desirable?"

Gabriel turned his face away again, forcibly and reluctantly. "Yes!" he hissed. "Very beautiful and very desirable."

"Then make love to me," I begged.

He looked at me for a second as though contemplating it, but pulled away completely. "Don't," he said. "Never beg for what you want."

"What should I do then, Gabriel? I love you so much. I'm going crazy…"

"Take what you want," Gabriel said. "Demand it."

It sunk in then. At that moment, I took more steps than I did in the last hour to pull Gabriel back to me, crushing my lips to his, and demanding him to kiss me back.

I kept kissing him until he began kissing me back, taking control of my lips with his. My hands reached over to the front of his pants, stroking his hard bulge.

"Fuck," Gabriel muttered. His arms swept under my knees lifting me high as he walked quickly into his casa and into his bedroom, depositing me onto his large and luxurious silk-covered bed. "I'm helpless to your demands, Baby Girl," Gabriel said.

"Then make love to me," I said.

Chapter 4

<u>Calla</u>
Age 21
Present Day
Paris, France

After the first assignment to assassinate the crime boss in England went so successfully, I took on another assignment to eliminate a terrorist who was now staying in France. Like my last assignment, I had settled into the location near my target, renting a modest apartment in Paris and quickly assimilating into local life.

I was a student of art, and I would set up my easel wherever and whenever the muse would hit me. Offering the perfect cover, I would be able to observe the daily routine of my target and monitor his activities without any suspicions.

Sipping a latte one day at my favorite café, I received a text from Gabriel, who gave me my assignment, a feat I had to wrestle him into after I found out he was a one-man vigilante. He was once one of the world's best hitmen. He had no alliance to any country, was already wealthy beyond belief thanks to an inheritance from his late aristocratic parents, and he didn't need to earn a living but made one in finance during the day and a vigilante at night. Like Batman, he was into justice, but instead of trying to save everyone, he chose his assignments voluntarily.

"Trust me, Baby Girl," he had said, "You don't want to get into this if you have other options. It isn't a living, it's a purpose and a reason."

"Well," I said, "I do have a purpose and a reason. I want to avenge my parents, and the damage their killer did to me. I want to avenge everyone who he hurt and destroyed."

Gabriel looked pained as he gazed at me. "It isn't the kind of life I wished to see you having, Baby Girl," he said. "I want to see you pampered every inch of your beautiful body, taken care of by me, and made love to every single night."

"If you have a strong sense of justice, I do too," I said. "I will be careful. I will be discrete. No one would ever suspect me."

Gabriel had looked me over, scrutinizing me like I was being examined for enlistment into the army. Finally, he nodded and said, "You are right. No one would suspect you."

"I look more like a victim than an assassin, don't I?" I asked.

"More like a princess," Gabriel said. "My beautiful princess who could not bear to see the sight of blood."

"Good cover," I said.

"Yes," Gabriel agreed. Not long after that conversation, when my body had healed, and I was able to run, climb, jump, and fight; we began my training as an assassin.

It had been a full year since then, and now I was on my second assignment. A man so dangerous and so diabolical, he could take out millions of people around the world. Instead of diplomacy, he used fear and terrorism to force people to comply with his demands.

Now I was looking at Gabriel's text. It was in code, and was the one word I had been waiting all month long for in order to act.

Kraken.

I finished my latte, picked up a fresh baked baguette, paid, and left the café. Instead of going straight to my apartment, I walked over to the back alleyway of the café.

In a hiding place behind two loose bricks, I pulled out a baguette bag to encase my short-barreled rifle. I attached a sound suppressor to the end of the barrel, took out the rest of my fresh baguette, turned it around and shoved it back into its bag with the untouched round end sticking out as a disguise.

I reversed my bright red trench coat into the more subdue beige side, pulled my hair into a ponytail, and pulled out a hat to hide my face. In Paris, any fashion statement was fine, especially hats.

Carrying my two bags of baguette, I walked over to the building my target was staying at and waited.

*****

My legs were almost asleep standing at the side of the building by the time *Mr. Slimeball* walked out, lighting a cigar.

The sky had darkened, but it was still a nice warm night.

Mr. Slimeball looked over at me, and I smiled.

"Bonjour," I said.

He nodded and began walking.

I walked a little behind him as if I were simply taking a stroll from the café to home. When we walked past an alleyway, I pretended to trip so I would fall into him, pushing him into the dark alley.

Now out of plain sight, I pulled out my rifle, ready to blast into him, when I heard him scream.

In the shadows of the dark, I saw some movement, and heard a swish of air and the *barely there* footsteps. It was so dark, I almost tripped over Mr. Slimeball when I got up and looked down, shining the light of my phone at him.

His throat had been slit from ear to ear. Clean.

Damn.

From the distance, I heard the sound of running and voices.

Mr. Slimeball's men.

I quickly walked out of the alleyway, right before two large men headed into alley. They were so close, and I was still in shock seeing that someone else had taken out Mr. Slimeball before I could, and they did it right out from under me.

"That girl!" someone shouted from the alleyway.

Fuck. I no longer had a cover. It didn't matter. I was the last person they saw coming out of the alleyway. I began running as fast as I could in my boots down each street, trying to lose them.

But my legs were stiff from standing for hours, and I was getting winded.

"There!" one of the nearby men said, as I stopped for a moment behind a wall to catch my breath.

"When I get her…" the other one said.

They rounded the corner, and I punched one of them in the face before kicking the other one in the knees. I began running again, but they caught me, and punched me in the stomach, catching the side of my ribs, causing me to fall to my knees.

"You are going to pay for what you did," the short one sneered, walking up to me and pulling my hair back to get me to face him.

I spat into his eyes, and he let go of my hair, just as I got up on my legs and punched him under his chin, sending his head back.

His friend was already on top of me, knocking me down with his weight. "In another time and another place, I would find you hot and fuck you, but…" I slammed my knee into his groin as hard as I could, causing him to roll over in pain.

Then I was off running again.

Until I hit a dead end.

"There's the bitch," the taller one said.

"I'm going to slit her throat from ear to ear like what she did to Korgar."

I was cornered with nowhere to go as they approached me, one of them holding a large knife.

They were a few feet away now.

I had one of my baguette bags with me still.

As I leveled the bag towards them, like a weapon, I said, "Stop or I'll blow your head off."

One of them laughed. "You can't tell me that's a gun."

"Try me," I said.

They looked at each other. Then in a flash, one of them charged at me to my right, while the other came at me straight ahead.

I pulled the bag down and pulled the trigger, shooting the one charging me straight ahead in the chest.

"Told you," I shouted, turning to shoot the second one in the head.

I was about to shoot the first victim again to eliminate witnesses when I heard shouting.

Walking as fast as I could, I slipped out of the street and into the darkness like a shadow…my heart pounding so hard, I could barely breathe.

Chapter 5

<u>Calla</u>
Age 21
Present Day – 2 Days Later
Casa Capri

"I almost had him," I said, taking the ice pack Gabriel handed to me. He sat down next to me in bed and rubbed onto my bruises a homemade ointment made of mysterious herbs grown on his island.

I winced as his gentle fingers lightly touched bruises along my ribs. "Ouch," I muttered.

"My poor Baby Girl," Gabriel said, "It hurts me to see you so bruised and battered. You shouldn't have taken this assignment."

"I was over-confident," I said. "I thought it'd be like the first assignment where I could blend into the night like you taught me. But those guys… they got a lucky break, catching me when I was unprepared, thrown off my plan."

"Nothing goes according to plan in this line of work, Baby Girl," Gabriel said.

"As long as you've been in it," I said, "has it ever gone smoothly?"

"My parents were killed ten years ago when I was 19, close to your age when you lost yours," Gabriel said. "Since that day, nothing about avenging them has gone smoothly. Even if things looked like it had gone smoothly, it is always difficult."

I looked into Gabriel's beautiful blue eyes. My poor beautiful man. I pulled his face close to me to kiss him. "Your heart…you still feel something when you complete an assignment."

Gabriel's eyes froze for a second and said, "You're not human if you don't. My parents were brutally murdered, and I saw it all. That was something you can never forget."

"No, you can't, and you shouldn't," I said. "You are justified for your anger, for your mission, Gabriel."

"But this is *my* mission, Baby Girl. You should not take it upon yourself to assassinate those who had a hand in murdering my parents. It is too dangerous."

"It was an opportunity, and I took it," I said.

"Unfortunately it was, and I couldn't stop you from it. When you put your head to it, you can accomplish anything, Baby Girl. I knew that when I first laid eyes on you. You are a survivor…the lone survivor of a boating accident that killed your family. You should have died in that accident, but you survived. That was a sign, Baby Girl."

"Of what, Gabriel?" I asked.

"For you to live," he said. "And you must continue to live. You were meant to, not taking risks with these assignments."

"Gabriel, Gabriel, Gabriel," I said, kissing his cheeks, his eyes, and his lips. "Please don't worry about me. I accomplished my mission and came out alive, didn't I?"

"Barely," Gabriel said. "Someone else assassinated the target, and you took the fall. You spent months preparing for this assignment, and when the time came to act, you left yourself wide open, standing in front of the target's building, waiting for him to come out."

"I was in disguise and pretending to be waiting for a friend to arrive in front of the apartments."

"Suspiciously waiting for a friend while holding two baguette bags? No one does that in Paris. When you buy fresh baguettes, you are in a hurry to go home to consume them, not wait for hours holding them just to have them grow cold and hard to eat."

"I have no choice, Gabriel," I said. "My target was supposed to come out of the building around that time, but he didn't. So there was a change of plans."

"Yes, like I said, things don't usually go as planned but you could have chosen a less conspicuous way to wait. At that moment, you could have walked away from the scene, and go further away to observe and wait from a less obvious distance, like return to the café or go to a shop or the park across from the apartment, sit on the bench there and pretend to read a book while eating the baguette."

"I wanted to be close enough to bump into him. I didn't want to miss the opportunity to close in on him, especially if he had his bodyguards with him."

"Even more so that you stay further away. If he had his bodyguards with him right as he left the building, you wouldn't even get close enough to kill him. And you would expose yourself to them all, losing the element of surprise," Gabriel said.

"That's why I wanted to be right there, if he had just stepped outside of his compound, to get a smoke and to take a short walk. Mr. Slimeball had been cooped up for weeks in that building, no doubt, with his bodyguards that he probably wanted to get some fresh air on his own. That was why I figured he would be without his bodyguards."

Gabriel's concerned face broke out into a smile. "Lucky for you, you figured right."

"But I didn't anticipate some other assassin coming into the picture and taking my target from under me," I said.

"No," Gabriel said. "That was unexpected, but then again, always expect the unexpected in this game. When things are going too smoothly, expect something else to happen."

"I did, but not like that," I said. "I thought I was the only one tailing him."

"He had many enemies," Gabriel said. "Did you get a chance to see the assassin?"

"It was too dark, and I've never seen anyone come in and out of a place like some kind of ghostly ninja."

"No doubt, your assassin thief is very experienced," Gabriel said.

"I want to get him back," I said. "He stole my target right from under me. I tailed my target for months, set him up to be in that alley away from his bodyguards, if only for minutes, then he stole him from right under me. That thief, that…"

Gabriel started laughing. "If you could see yourself right now, Baby Girl. You're red with anger, but still looked like a sweet angel, and you're talking about assassinating someone."

"A very very bad and dangerous man whose existence would cause more and more people to die. Slimeball's history is like a horror novel. He had entire families and their lineage wiped out, buried with no gravestones, and that's only the tip of the iceberg with what is known about him. Who knows how many more he would kill if he lived on?"

"Well, Baby Girl," Gabriel said, "I know I can't talk you out of doing what you want to do so I can only hope you can take care of yourself better and to be able to hone your instincts so you'd make smarter decisions."

"What are you saying, Gabriel?"

Gabriel looked at me and said, "You're staying with me for a while longer until you're better and also better trained."

I couldn't help grinning widely. "I love every opportunity to be with you, Gabriel," I said. "I will stay longer. I love you so much."

Chapter 6

<u>Calla</u>
Age 20
Past
Casa Capri

The wind from the breeze that flowed sweetly through the palm trees and open fields of the Isle of Capri or affectionately known to me as Gabriel's Island, whipped my long dark hair like a halo of black flame as I tore through the valley riding on Angelica, my white mare, who Gabriel presented to me on my 20th birthday, not too long ago. It had already been a full year since I landed at Gabriel's

Island. One year that meant more to me than any other year. It was the only year I remembered up to now.

With a snap of my wrist, I unleashed an arrow from my bow, straight through the center of each target.

With a zing and a twist of my wrist, the last target in the field was punctured straight through the bullseye. I hopped down off Angelica, ran across a field trying to dodge the shots of fire aimed at me from Gabriel's men. Running, ducking, and rolling to each bush, to hide behind, I finally crossed through the field as paint from paintball guns were fired at me.

Having cleared the field, I climbed up a wall with the rock-climbing equipment already attached to the wall, and ran towards an old warehouse where I had to scale a building to an open window.

Once there, I jumped in, but noticed an object flying toward me. I ducked quickly and gasped as I realized I avoided being decapitated by a flying ax.

This game was becoming too real.

With my flashlight, I searched the room. More than a warehouse, this room was full of paintings. Fine art portraits and landscapes adorned the walls like a gallery. Was this where Gabriel hid his collection? He was a billionaire on his own right after entering the financial sector straight out of Cambridge University. He was a *wunderkind*. He had many wealthy and powerful clients, who he made wealthier and more powerful. Of course these paintings must be real.

But the Mona Lisa? What was a museum piece like that doing here? Surely it could not be the genuine art. Something was off about the painting being amongst genuine paintings of art in this gallery. It did not fit with the rest.

I walked over and gently removed Mona Lisa's painting off the wall, and brought it to a table nearby. The painting looked just like the real artwork, displayed in the Louvre in Paris. If a replica, it was one of the best. I turned the painting backwards and took out my pocket knife, opening the blade to cut open the back at the seam.

"Voila!" I exclaimed, finding a key.

Snatching the key, looked around the room. What object in this room required a key to open?

I walked around the room, noticing some antique furniture. Not only were they old, but they were magnificent as though they once belonged in a palace. Gilded gold benches, intricately carved console tables, and in the corner stood a golden grandfather clock as wide as a football receiver and tall as a basketball player. The clock face was inlaid with ivory and jade, and in the center was a small keyhole.

I opened the cover of the clock face and slid my key in, holding my breath as I twisted it. With a click, the clock face opened, and in the hollow hiding place behind was a box.

I took the box out and opened it. In the center was a pair of diamond earrings. And a Note. From Gabriel.

Congratulations on completing this game so successfully. You have found your prize for solving the mystery. A gift for your anniversary of being here with me. I am so proud of you. I love you, Baby Girl.

Gabriel appeared from behind a secret door. Gabriel was dressed in a beautiful blue silk suit, and walked toward me. His black mask over his eyes had made him sexier than I had ever seen him.

He was immediately on me, his mouth on mine kissing me so deeply and passionately, I couldn't breathe. With a deep groan, he back me onto the table where the Mona Lisa replica laid, pushed it off the table, and laid me down, tearing off my shirt first while kissing down my neck to my breasts and then my stomach.

With a flick of his hands, he ripped off my shorts, and peeled my panties off. His mouth on me as his fingers dipped into me, hitting my sensitive nerve just right.

"Oh Gabriel," I moaned. "Oh yes!" I grabbed his soft silky black hair and gently scratched his head. He was the most beautiful man I had ever seen. The sexiest as well.

"You were like a goddess today, Baby Girl," Gabriel groaned. "Riding through the fields like a warrior princess, confidently eluding the shots from my men in the field, scaling the walls like a siren. Then you found the diamond earrings I had wanted to give you for so long." He bit me hard on my clit before I shuddered.

I moaned as I climaxed, but he swallowed my moan kissing me with a fervor as he entered me with one fell swoop. I cried out in his mouth as the pleasure was so intense.

"So fucking sexy and smart, Baby Girl," Gabriel grunted, thrusting into me relentlessly and continuously until we both cried out in ecstasy.

"I love you, Gabriel," I kissed him after we settled down. "I'm yours. Yours forever."

"Mine," Gabriel sighed. "My Baby Girl."

Chapter 7

<u>Calla</u>
Age 21
Present Day
Casa Capri

I was back in Gabriel's bed, back in the care of his loving and caring arms.

"Being away from you is torture," I told him as I kissed his temple and his lips.

"Then don't take assignments that require you to travel away from me, Baby Girl," he said.

"You can't expect me to just remain here at the island and do nothing," I said.

"Do nothing?" Gabriel asked, kissing me and moving his hands down underneath my comforter to rub my folds.

I closed my eyes as I relished the pleasure of his fingers on me.

Gabriel chuckled as I began wriggling and bucking with need. "Gabriel, I need you."

"I thought you said you find being at the island not to your liking," he said.

"Gabriel," I moaned now tearing off the comforter and exposing my breasts to him. He loved my round breasts. When he said I was healing from my accident, my breasts did not need any surgery since they were perfect as they were, the kind women aspire to have at plastic surgeons' offices.

Gabriel's eyes filled with lust and he bent down to take my nipples into his mouth, sucking on them before licking them.

"Ohh Gabriel," I moaned, "That's good. So good. Now fuck me, please."

"Good things come to those who wait," he said between licking my nipples.

I reached down and pulled his pajama pants down, grabbing his large veiny cock. Stroking it, I pushed Gabriel down to his back on the bed before I took his cock into my mouth.

"Oh Baby Girl," Gabriel groaned. "That feels so good."

I kept my eyes on his as I went up and down his cock, licking the tip before taking it all in.

"Fuck, that's so sexy," Gabriel groaned.

I continued sucking on him until he started bucking.

"I'm going to come," Gabriel said.

"Come, then," I said. "I want you."

He groaned, tensed, and let go, spilling into my mouth as I swallowed.

When he was sated, he pushed me down on the bed, licked and teased my folds until I was dripping before he pushed into me, fucking me hard and relentlessly, pounding into me so I could feel every stroke.

"God, Gabriel," I moaned. "Pound me so hard I can feel it through my pain."

"Yes, Baby Girl," he grunted, relentlessly fucking me until I exploded along with him.

"Only you," I cried out. "My legs were numbed until you fucked me into feeling them again. Only you can give it to me that hard."

"Yes, Baby Girl," Gabriel smiled, looking at me. "I gave life back to you," he said. "It is good that you remember it."

Chapter 8

<u>Calla</u>
2 Weeks Later - Age 21
Casa Capri

I was once again in the fields of Gabriel's Island, but blindfolded and surrounded by two of Gabriel's men. I didn't know any of them personally since they came and went without my knowledge. They were also kept from me, as though I were Gabriel's hidden secret.

But when it came to training, Gabriel brought a few of his trusted guards to help. Now I could sense there were about 3 or 4 of them. Two of them to my right, and one in front of me while another was to my left.

How I knew that, I did not exactly know except by instinct and the ability to feel their presence.

A slight movement and a cool breeze came at me from the right. I ducked and swept the ground with my leg, knocking one of the men down to the ground. From there, I could feel the weighted ground to my right where he had fallen, jumped on top of him, and punched hard. My knuckles hit cartilage, and I heard a crack before a scream. I had broken the man's nose.

"Sorry," I said. It was practice, and I shouldn't have hit so hard.

"Okay," Gabriel's voice shouted. "Enough for the day. Guys, go to the kitchen and get dinner from the Chef."

"Yes, Sir," the men said.

I took off my blindfold and looked around. There were four men retreating, just as I had guessed.

"Impressive for a first timer," Gabriel said.

"I trusted my instincts," I said.

"Good instincts," Gabriel said, walking around me. "How many men did you guess?"

"Four," I said. "And I was right."

Gabriel shook his head. "No, you missed one more."

I looked at Gabriel and said, "But I saw four guys walking back to the Casa."

"But you still missed one, and that one man you missed could be the very one who would kill you."

I looked down and saw that Gabriel's boots were wet, just like his men's. "You," I said. "You were circling me, too."

"Yes, but a few steps behind each of them."

"Like a phantom," I said.

"Bingo," Gabriel said.

"You could feel four, but you couldn't see behind them for the fifth guy or maybe sixth or seventh."

"I was fighting blind," I said. "How could I possibly see if there were more men?"

"It isn't easy," Gabriel said, "But you do hone your instincts to notice more of your environment. It's what soldiers do, Baby Girl. Even in the dark."

I looked down, realizing how much I didn't know yet.

"So you see, it isn't about just being able to carry a gun, disguise yourself, or track someone's whereabouts," Gabriel said. "It's about that moment when you are caught completely by surprise and all you have to rely on are your instincts."

"Like what happened to me with the Phantom," I said.

"Exactly," Gabriel said.

He must have seen how disappointed I was in myself so he placed his arm around my shoulder. "Baby Girl," he kissed me on my forehead. "Don't beat yourself over it. Most people don't have half the amount of fighting instincts you've shown today. You will develop more of it over time and experience. It took me years to get to where you are, Baby Girl, until I found my motivation."

"Your parents," I said.

"Yes," Gabriel nodded. "My only motivation. It kept me alive all the times I thought I didn't want to go on."

"What memories do you have of your parents?" I asked.

"Many. Mostly happy ones, Baby Girl. You see, I lived a fairy tale life with my parents. I was their only son and they adored me. I knew nothing else but complete unconditional love."

"That golden grandfather clock and those paintings in that building…they belonged to them, didn't they?"

"Yes, the remainders from my parents' estate. We lost the house, we lost almost everything when they came for them…my parents. Then they killed them in front of me, while I watched helplessly." Gabriel's eyes glistened.

"You kept that building with everything in there as a reminder," I said.

Gabriel nodded. "Of the justice I promised them."

"And your mask?" I asked. I never dared to ask before, but something about the way Gabriel was acting made me feel it was the right time.

"They let me live," Gabriel said slowly, "but they left me with a reminder of what they could do to me if I ever dared to try anything,"

I wanted to see what was underneath his mask. I knew how horrific it was, I would still find him the most beautiful man alive.

"Can I see you without your mask?" I asked. "Perhaps one day."

Gabriel turned away. "No, you cannot. It is a scar that I wear…shamefully."

"It doesn't matter, Gabriel," I said. "I'll love you just the same. You're the most beautiful man I've ever known. Inside and out. You're perfect."

"I may have been known for my looks before," Gabriel said, "living the life of an aristocratic playboy but when they took everything away from me, even my dignity; I felt hideous like a monster. So I became one. I fled my parents' home to my mother's family's island…this one, and lived like a hermit. Only those who worked the fields, those who work at the Casa, and a handful of bodyguards accompany me on this island live or work on this island with me. However, I had no one here who gave me a sense of family, of hope, of love. Until I saw your lifeless half-drowned body on the rocks below."

My eyes were watering as I took his face between my hands and kissed him.

"I saw me in you, Baby Girl," Gabriel said. "You had lost everything too, including your memory. And your body was broken, like my soul. For the first time in so long, I felt something."

"I'm good for you," I said. "Admit it, Masked Lover. Admit it!" I kissed him again.

"You're a good for nothing," Gabriel joked.

"No, I'm good for you," I said, kissing him again but more passionately.

"Oh yeah?" Gabriel asked. He threw me to the ground, and before you knew it, we were making love in the fields as the sky darken into night.

Chapter 9

<u>Calla</u>
Age 21
New York City, New York

A few weeks had passed and I was on another assignment. This time it was in the Gotham-like city of New York.

I had recovered fully and was confident enough after being trained by Gabriel in the art of fighting in the dark and possibly dealing with surprises like what happened in France. This time, my assignment was to take down a pedophile politician in New York City.

My cover was that of a schoolgirl. Dressed as a young schoolgirl at a political fundraiser, which was for raising funds to build a new addition to a prep school, I was supposed to be the student who would be introducing him at the fundraiser.

Walking up to the stage, I looked like a sweet, unsuspecting student. "We are so honored to have Congressman Slamberg here to talk about the benefits of your funds for use at St. Claire Prep," I said beaming at the Congressman.

The blonde middle-aged man made his way toward the platform, looked me up and down like he was checking me out, and then faced the audience.

What a pervert. How dare he look at me like that while standing in front of this huge crowd.

He made a short speech and ended the fundraiser like he couldn't wait to get out. But as I made my way off the platform and down to the ground floor, he stopped me and said, "You did a great job introducing me. You might have a career in politics one day."

I smiled demurely. "Really?"

"Yes, and if you want to know the secrets on how to get ahead in this cutthroat world, meet me in the principal's office in about 15 minutes."

"Okay," I said and walked away. I could feel his grotesque eyes burning on my rear.

A few minutes later, I walked into the principal's office, and Congressman Slamberg was wearing only his socks and shoes. Naked and casually leaning against the principal's desk, he was stroking himself with a lecherous smile on his face.

"Come here, sweet stuff," he said, his tongue hanging out of the side of his mouth.

I slowly walked over, assuming a shy school girl manner. I got close enough to take out the sharp dagger hidden behind my back, hidden in a belt sheath, ready to cut off his dick and then slit his throat. But as I was about to plunge my dagger into him, he awkwardly fell backward onto the desk. Dead. A bullet through his eyes.

I turned around behind me, and noticed a figure all in black, dressed like the Phantom assassin who took my target back in France. "You again," I shouted.

He was standing outside the building at the window he was perched to take the kill shot. I ran to the window, breaking the remaining glass fragments around the window frame with a broomstick. I leaped through it, landing on my feet below. He was just standing there as if he were waiting for me to confront him.

"Who are you? Why are you killing my targets?" I asked.

"They're mine, too. Free for the taking, School Girl," he said. His voice was distorted behind his masked face, so I couldn't hear his real voice.

"No, they're not..." I said. "I specifically signed up for those two..."

"Tough breaks, Kid," the assassin said. "When there's a call out, it's first come, first served."

"But..."

"See you at your next assignment, Kid," he said taking off.

I wanted to chase him, but it was no use. In a flash, he was gone.

Chapter 10

<u>Calla</u>
Age 21
Casa Capri

I couldn't wait to get back to Gabriel and Casa Capri, ashamed that I had been made a fool of twice by the Phantom assassin.

Gabriel was working in his office at the Casa, talking on the phone with some clients. Although he no longer worked in the financial industry, he still took on major clients.

I was pacing back and forth, too angry at the Phantom assassin. The man was purposely knocking off my targets before I could get to them. I led my target to where they were supposed to be, and then the Phantom would steal them away from me, reaping the rewards, while I became the culprit.

When Gabriel got off the phone and came toward me, he had a look on his face of pure sympathy and love. "Baby Girl, what happened?"

"The Phantom strikes again," I said.

"He took your target?"

"Right from under me," I said.

"Irritating," Gabriel said.

"More than irritating," I said. "Downright insulting and shameless. He deliberately said they're for his taking."

"Wow, shameless," Gabriel said.

"Gabriel," I sank into his arms, "Teach me to beat this guy."

"What do you want me to teach, Baby Girl? How to act faster? How to be more aware of your surroundings? How sometimes you don't need to set up a cover, but to just get it done?"

"So you're telling me I shouldn't spend my time assuming a cover and spy-like work?"

"It may pay off but when you don't have much time, you just get it done."

"But shouldn't there be some kind of assassin ethics?" I asked.

"I wasn't aware there were any," Gabriel said. "I operate only to avenge my parents and bring them justice. Justice to me is absolute. I'm in it for personal reasons, never for professional, like your rival. You have to ask yourself why you are in it, if you go against a professional. If it's a vendetta, then you make sure you get the target. If it's professional, then I guess there's professional courtesy."

"I just want to avenge my parents' death and take down horrible human beings like the ones who killed them," I said.

Gabriel kissed me and kept kissing me, saying, "I missed tasting your lips, Baby Girl. I missed tasting you."

He had me against the wall of the hallway between his office and the living room, with my arms raised and pinned at the wrist by one of his hands. "Fuck me, Gabriel," I said. "I need you."

He plunged deep into me, rocking me up the wall and continued fucking me until we were spent and exhausted.

Chapter 11

<u>Calla</u>
Age 21
Casa Capri

Gabriel had me up bright and early in the morning as we ate breakfast out on the patio overlooking the ocean.

"That was where I spotted you," Gabriel said pointing to an area in the distance.

"In the ocean, swimming?" I asked.

"No," Gabriel said. "On a yacht. A luxury yacht," Gabriel smiled. "You knew how to enjoy luxury, Baby Girl. Your parents owned the yacht, and you were on it, standing like a goddess at the helm."

I was speechless. Gabriel had always said he found me on the rocky shores of his island, but I never heard him say he saw me and my parents on a luxury yacht.

"I was with my parents?" I asked.

"I assume they were your parents," Gabriel said. "Do you remember their faces?"

I tried to remember, but shook my head.

Gabriel didn't seem too upset or too happy about it either. "Then you wouldn't know, couldn't tell who they were."

"No," I said. "I couldn't tell."

"Well," Gabriel said, "I first spotted you on the yacht. Then all of a sudden, the yacht exploded, and you must have fallen off the yacht in the explosion and made it to the shores of my island."

"And you took me in," I said.

"I had to," Gabriel said.

"It's fate, Gabriel," I said. "We were meant to meet."

"Yes," Gabriel said. "Yes. And today, we won't need you to practice in the fields. We're going to talk our way for your training, through scenarios."

"Why?" I asked.

"No amount of physical training will help you defeat the Phantom," Gabriel said. "It's all mental," he said, tapping his temple.

Gabriel continued. "When did the Phantom show up? After you lured your target to a specific spot, it seems that the Phantom had already beaten you to it. He must have known where you would end up. He shows up ready and prepared to hit his mark, correct?"

I nodded. "Of course, that was why. But how could he figure where I would lure them?" I asked.

"It is because the Phantom already knew what you would do. He knows how you think. He already knew your moves like a chess game, so he anticipated your next move. That just means you either have to change your methodology and or you had to anticipate the Phantom's moves ahead of time," Gabriel concluded, taking a sip from his cup of coffee.

My mouth was open. "Why and how is it that a man your age, late 20s can be so wise?" I asked.

"I've experienced a lot of things at an early age, Baby Girl," Gabriel said. "Many awful things. It makes a person grow up fast."

I was truly impressed how Gabriel knew exactly how to figure out my opponent. I took his hand and said, "I still have so much to learn from you. You're like a chess master, and I needed to know how to think like you."

Gabriel smiled at me and leaned over to kiss me. "I have no doubt you will one day, and when that day comes, I would be willing to step aside as *Master*."

Chapter 12

<u>Calla</u>
Age 21
A month later
Miami, Florida

One month later, I felt ready to take on another assignment. I was ready to take on Phantom assassin as well. Gabriel stepped in and said this one was personal. It was one of the persons heavily responsible for the deaths of his parents, and he had finally located him.

The target lived in a beach house in Miami so the best way to get to him would be by boat. Although Gabriel told me I shouldn't plan on using a cover or having an extensive stake out, but to go in and get it done; I still wanted to have a cover and to observe the target from afar.

His name was Wilson Kramer, and he was an attorney with a large law firm. I wondered what he did to end up being Gabriel's personal target? He lived alone, and he didn't appear to have a family, although he did have some family photos in his beach house. I couldn't get close enough to see, nor could I see the details of the photos through my telephoto lens.

For my stake out, I rented a sail boat and sat anonymously in the harbor. I had a good view of his living room, kitchen, and front door. And after just a week of observations, he never used curtains or blinds to shutter his windows.

Bad move, Mr. Kramer. Bad people and lookie-loos can easily see inside your house, what you do all day, and plan diabolical things.

I didn't know much about the white-haired man in his sixties, but he did not strike me as the typical criminal, terrorist, corrupt politician, and pedophiliac who we would typically take down. In fact, the man seemed normal. Same routine every morning. Same routine every night. Eating alone at his dining table. Even glancing down at a photo while he ate.

One time I caught him sobbing while he sat on the toilet, not bothering to close the door. He had no idea I was watching.

Another time, I saw him watching a children's show while holding a worn-looking teddy bear. I didn't want to look him up for fear of getting too attached to a target, but somehow his name, Kramer, sounded familiar.

Was he famous? Well-known enough to be a household name?

I didn't want to find out. A target was a target, and in this case, if Gabriel wanted him dead, there must have been a valid reason. And knowing Gabriel, the only reason was to avenge the deaths of his parents.

I loved and trusted Gabriel enough to follow through with what he wanted me to do. He taught me everything, and he gave me everything.

Soon, the time was right, and I was going to just get it done. That night, I sailed my boat into his dock, and walked up to the glass patio of his house. It was unlocked.

As if Kramer was expecting me.

I gulped. Was he armed? Did he have a trap set up for me?

I pulled out my gun, ready for anything. Gabriel had trained me well. I was prepared for whatever Kramer had in store.

What I didn't expected was this.

Chapter 13

<u>Calla</u>
Age 21
Miami, Florida
Kramer's House

Kramer was sitting in his favorite arm chair reading a book. A pink hardcover book that a little girl would have.

He had a smile on his face as he read the book, *A Little Girl's Bible Stories*.

"My little girl's book," he said. "My lost little girl's book. Thank you for letting me read it one last time."

I thought he was talking to me, but it was someone else.

To the right of the man, just barely out of my view was the Phantom assassin. With a gun pointed at Wilson Kramer's head.

Not again. The Phantom assassin had beaten me to my target. A rage filled me like I had never experienced before. He was not going to be the first to assassinate my targets. He was not going to humiliate me again and make me look like a fool.

The honor of my parents' names and my vengeance for them depended on it.

Without even looking at my target, I shot him in between the eyes, as I sneered at the Phantom assassin.

Kramer's head fell back, and he was dead.

I heard a diabolical chuckling coming from the side of the dead man. The Phantom assassin was laughing. Hysterically. "Now why did you go ahead and do that?"

He was wearing a black mask like last time. Like all the times I had met him. And his voice wasn't muffled any longer.

It was melodic, rich, and very familiar.

I didn't care that he had a gun on him. I walked right up to him and tore his mask off him.

He didn't even blink his blue eyes as he stared at me with eyes I had gazed so lovingly into. They were the most mesmerizing eyes I had ever seen. Then he said, "I've been waiting for this moment for so long, Baby Girl."

Gabriel.

My heart dropped as I looked around Wilson Kramer's beach house, now from within, instead of outside through a telephoto lens.

There were pictures. Lots of pictures of a little girl with dark flowing hair and blue eyes. Artwork and handprints hanging on the walls.

My eyes blinked several times as I looked at each artwork in horror.

They were all signed in child-like scribbles with the signature.

CALLA

I looked to Gabriel, my eyes wide in horror. "What have I done?" I asked.

Gabriel was not the same man I knew at Casa Capri. He was now unmasked, and his scar was horrific. No wonder why he didn't want me to see it. Written across the bottom of his eyes were the words carved deeply into his flesh, "The Devil".

Gabriel said, "I told you you wouldn't want to see me without my mask."

"Gabriel," I cried. "What's all this?"

"Calla," Gabriel said. "Your family home. It's written all over the place. Don't you recognize it?"

I walked over to one of the photos framed in a "Home Sweet Home" picture frame. One of a beautiful woman with dark hair, Wilson Kramer, and a girl in a cap and gown. Me.

Gabriel was beaming. "This is sweeter than I had imagined."

"I don't understand…"

"Baby Girl, you just killed your own father."

Baby Girl (Baby Girl #1)

Epilogue

<u>Calla</u>

One Year Later

The only thing I remembered was my name: Calla, which meant *Beauty* in Greek. My Greek mother had chosen the name as she once told me that I was their miracle baby girl they were foretold to have one day.

Being older parents, my mother and father thought they would be childless since they could not have children when they were younger despite trying for years. They tried every method to have children, and in the end, I was born through a surrogate.

My parents cherished me, and I grew up in a beautiful beach house where my mother would take me out on the beach and help me build sand castles. Meanwhile, my father worked at his law firm. Life growing up with my parents was like a fairy tale, and I loved my parents with all my heart.

Having the most wonderful parents in the world, they took me on a summer vacation one day, sailing on a yacht we rented to sail through the Mediterranean on my 19th birthday after returning from my first year in college. I wanted an adventure and I had always wanted to see the Mediterranean countries and islands.

But as we came closer to a small private island, the yacht was shot at with a rocket launcher, blasting it to pieces, and throwing my father, mother, and me out to sea.

Apparently my father, Wilson Kramer had survived. And I had survived. But my mother Marnie Kramer did not. Her whereabouts were unknown. And I, not remembering who I was, was also thought to be dead, drowned at sea.

It took me a long time to find out the truth about my family. I didn't quite regain all my memories of them, but after the shock of what happened, and how Gabriel had played this game with me the entire time, it was the kind of electric shock I needed to jog my memories.

My memories were slowly coming back, mingled with my memories of Gabriel on the Isle of Capri and at Casa Capri where I spent blissful days of love and lust with the man I thought I knew. Only to know that instead of the Angel of the Isle, he was the Devil.

He was my teacher and my lover. He taught me well… to find justice. To avenge my parents. Gabriel, I would be coming after you soon.

Baby Girl (Baby Girl #1)

Calla and Gabriel's story will continue in
Book 2 of Baby Girl Series.

Deadly Doll (Baby Girl #2)

https://www.amazon.com/dp/B08QCR3NQM

A DARK BULLY COLLEGE
ROMANCE
Deadly Doll
RABY GIRL SERIES #2
USA TODAY BESTSELLING AUTHOR
RACHEL ANGEL

A Note from Rachel Angel

Thank you for reading Baby Girl.

If you enjoyed it, please let others know by leaving a review.

Reviews are the lifeblood of authors like me. It helps keep the books you enjoy reading stay alive, much like supporting your local restaurant and shops.

That's the best support any author can ask for!

THANK YOU!

RACHEL ANGEL
Bio and Book Series

An international USA Today Bestselling author, Rachel Angel writes stories about Strong Feisty Women and the men they tame in RH, Bully Romances, Dark Romances, Fantasy, PNR, and sexy billionaire Romances. Rachel Angel is a pen name for a million-selling author who worked as an executive at Fortune 50 corporations, in legal and production at cable television channels and at the Walt Disney Corporation. Besides being a full time author with various pen names, she appears in front of the camera as a television host, voiceover artist, and is a frequent guest on top 15 National Radio as an authority on women's issues, the entertainment industry, and women empowerment. Her non-fiction books have been number one bestsellers, used by organizations such as the US Mental Health Association. Pushing the edge of romance, books published under Rachel Angel explores the hidden, dark, and even deepest desires of human romances, while featuring strong female leads.

BOOK SERIES

BAD BOY ROYALS OF KINGSBURY PREP
(Complete)
**RH New Adult/High School Bully Dark Contemporary
Romance – HEAT 4 out of 5**

Tempest and The Black Envelope (Books 1 and 2) with
Bonus and Clue on the Treasure
https://www.amazon.com/dp/B07Z44T1PF

Revenge

https://www.amazon.com/gp/product/B07SQP3HL3

Secret Princess
https://www.amazon.com/dp/B07YLHJ38K

Fallen Royals
https://www.amazon.com/dp/B07XXC625K

Reign of Rebels
https://www.amazon.com/dp/B07XM3FKW6

Link to Kingsbury Prep Series
https://www.amazon.com/gp/bookseries/B07S7ZVZWQ

Complete Series Box Set
https://www.amazon.com/gp/product/B08781CS94

Kingmakers of Kingsbury Series
RH Bully Fantasy Paranormal Shifter Fae
Romance – HEAT 4 out of 5

Long before there was an All-Royals Academy called Kingsbury Prep, there was the Kingmaker and her kings.

As Violet Kingsbury, I was born to be a kingmaker. In a time when wars were common and thrones were fought after, the only name that could bring about peace...the only man that could trump the decrees of kings was Kingsbury. The Kingmaker. But when the legendary Kingmaker is disposed, and the time of the Choosing has come, can I, the daughter

of The Kingmaker rise to take the place of my father? I am about to find out as the strongest, most capable, and most legendary princes across the lands come to challenge me for the Choosing including 4 of the most handsome princes who not only wants to win, but to want to win me, too:
Avery
Axel
Reggie
Ollie

*Becoming Kingmaker, even as The Kingmaker's daughter, will not be easy in a male world where ladies were supposed to be daMs.els who needed saving. To become Kingmaker, I will prove to all, especially the princes, that I am here to stay, and will be the one doing the saving. **Kingmakers of Kingsbury Series, Is a Reverse Harem Bully Romance with mixed genres elements, action, and mature scenes recommended for age 18 and up.*

Kingmaker's Kings (Book 1)
https://www.amazon.com/dp/B082QMNCW4
Kingmaker's Kiss (Book 2) (May 18, 2020)
https://www.amazon.com/gp/product/B084BZYW28

Kingmaker's Kill (Book 3) (July 28, 2020)
https://www.amazon.com/gp/product/B084BT8154

<u>HEARTBREAK FALLS</u>

RH Bully Dark New Adult/High School Romance Mystery – HEAT 4 out of 5

With a name like Heartbreak Falls, one didn't expect to find love at the new town I had moved to courtesy of my new stepfamily aka Mom's new husband and his sons.

Something was up with my new rich stepfather, his sons, and what happened to their last stepmother. Something was up with the entire town, which my

stepfamily seem to run. Along with the school where my stepbrothers reigned as cruel princes. All 3 of them were known as The Heartbreakers. Two were twins and my age, and then there was Tristan, the oldest. Gorgeous but god-awful hateful to me. What was up? I was about to find out...if I lived long enough.
***Heartbreak Falls is a RH Dark Bully Romance and mystery for 18 and up. It is YA/NA and has themes of bullying and sex. If that's fine with you, then dig in! Bully Me Not is book 1 of 5 and contains a cliffhanger.*
Bully Me Not

https://www.amazon.com/dp/B07XNQV36Q

Break Me Not
https://www.amazon.com/dp/B07XX7HZZZ

Dare Me Not
https://www.amazon.com/dp/B07Z4369V7

Destroy Me Not (June 29, 2020)
https://www.amazon.com/gp/product/B084C143VR

Love Me Not (September 28, 2020)
https://www.amazon.com/gp/product/B084BTRVYN

Baby Girl (Baby Girl #1)

HOUSE

RH Dark College New Adult Romance – HEAT 5 out of 5

It was his last will and testament.

For one week, four of us was to live together. Play nice to each other like we used to when we were kids.

Seb, Thomas, Ashford and me.

Baby Girl (Baby Girl #1)

Three of Mr. Keystone's sons and me, the maid's daughter.

All those years, the three sons bullied and ridiculed me because I was the maid's daughter.

So, why was I back? Why did I cared to be in the same house as those three tormentors?

Because I was in Mr. Keystone's will.

He had always been kind to me, even if his sons weren't, so I could only honor his wishes. And he was like a father to me, and didn't treat me like the maid's daughter. But as soon as I could, I left to go to college. Two years ago. Meanwhile, the boys went their separate ways, too. Estranged from each other.

So why was I here having to live in the same house with his sons for a week?

I don't know, but I'm about to find out, even if it meant my old adolescent feelings for all three of them might surface again. And if being in the mansion we called a house together might jog some memories of the wild nights we've had here.

It's just one week. I could survive that. Or could I?

***House is the first book in The House Series, which is a*

Reverse Harem Dark College Romance recommended for age 18+ due to mature themes.

House (The House Series, Book #1) (May 26, 2020)
https://www.amazon.com/gp/product/B0863Z36S5

Haven (The House Series, Book #2) (August 25, 2020)
https://www.amazon.com/gp/product/B087BFJWK5
Habit (The House Series, Book #3) (Nov. 2, 2020)
https://www.amazon.com/gp/product/B087B6MZDM
HEIRS (The House Series, Book #4) (Feb. 8, 2021)
https://www.amazon.com/gp/product/B087BCKS27
Haunt (The House Series, Book #5) (April 6, 2021)
https://www.amazon.com/gp/product/B087BGL27P
Home (The House Series, Book #6) (Nov, 2021)
https://www.amazon.com/gp/product/B08966PF77

FALLEN FAE ACADEMY

RH Bully Romance Fantasy Paranormal Fae – HEAT 4 out of 5

"At Fallen Fae Academy, the magic will either complete you or kill you."

My name is Harley, as in Harlequin. Plucked from my home from Las Vegas, NV, and placed into an University on an arts scholarship, suddenly I am the girl the four hottest and most popular boys have decided to "initiate".

This is no ordinary "hazing" ritual, and these boys are no ordinary boys.

This mysterious University looks like any ivy league campus, but it isn't. Step in and you are transported beyond your wildest imagination. I should be ecstatic being here. Except surviving "Initiation" is going to take everything I've got.

Don't let the beauty of the four fae boys fool you. They are as dangerous as they are beautiful. And underneath everything, runs a deep secret. One I need to find out before Initiation kills me.

They think a human is weak. They think I shouldn't be at this university. I'm about to prove them wrong.

**The Fallen Fae Series is a 6-book RH Academy College Bully Romance Series featuring a badass heroine, four deadly, striking fae princes, heart-pounding action, super steamy love scenes, and great romance.

Initiation: Year 1 Fallen Fae Academy Book 1
https://www.amazon.com/Initiation-Year-Academy-Reversed-Paranormal-ebook/dp/B07V9L8LHD

Baby Girl (Baby Girl #1)

Transformation: Year 2 Fallen Fae Academy Book 2
https://www.amazon.com/dp/B07WWFXVCH

Declaration: Year 3 Fallen Fae Academy Book 3
https://www.amazon.com/gp/product/B07XLMS.GDJ

Interruption War Year 3 (Fallen Fae Academy #4) (April 13, 2020)
https://www.amazon.com/dp/B0833JC8YJ

paperback version
https://www.amazon.com/Interruption-War-Year-Reversed-Paranormal/dp/B086Y5JYZG

Disruption (Fallen Fae Academy #5) (July 13, 2020)
https://www.amazon.com/dp/B084DB7F1B

Succession (Fallen Fae Academy Book #6) (October 19, 2020)
https://www.amazon.com/dp/B084D4VRCY

Fallen Fae Academy Box Set Part 1 (Books 1 -3)
https://www.amazon.com/gp/product/B08772LQFT

Rachel Angel

FALLEN FAE B. I. Series

RH Paranormal Romance Fantasy – HEAT 4 out of 5

Fae-ther Issues (Fallen Fae B.I. Book #1) Coming in 2021!

Now that it is changeling Harley's Ms.ion to find and capture the rogue dark fae her evil father has unleashed into the human world, Harley leaves the opulence of her mother's kingdom in the Faery RealMs. to return to her human adopted parents' home in Las Vegas to start her career as a trainee FBI agent. Piece of cake, isn't it, especially since she has finally discovered and mastered the powerful fae magic she went through the Fallen Fae Academy to learn. When a series of unusual murders show up along the Strip, and a close friend becomes the suspect, Harley would never have guess who would show up to give her some advice and clue to solve the murders…her evil dark fae wizard father. But could she trust him? Meanwhile the four princes from her Fallen Fae Academy days grapple with her decision to live in Las Vegas instead of assuming the throne of her kingdom in the Faery RealMs.

Fae-mous (Fallen Fae B.I. Book #2) (March 2021)

Harley's last case took her from casino to casino along the Las Vegas Strip in search of a killer who may have been a rogue dark fae, who wield a power she had yet to encounter. With the aid of her former classmates and still current lovers from Fallen Fae Academy, Harley devise a scheme to lure out the killer. Things become complicated when Harley and her guys discover the unusual murders before were a mere distraction from a bigger plot, her father and the rogue dark fae minions he had unleashed, had planned and had already set into motion…one that involves Las Vegas' former past as an Atomic bomb testing site to the beginning of the Apocalypse.

Fae-ful (Fallen Fae B.I. Book #3) (May 2021)

The clock is ticking. Harley and her guys must figure out the clues where the rogue dark fae army will unleash their dark magic and destroy the human race. Using the powers of all the kingdoMs. in the faery realMs., Harley and her four fae princes' powers converge to fight the power of the dark fae in the fight of their lifetimes.

<u>CRUEL PRINCES OF WYVERN ALL-BOYS ACADEMY</u>
(RH Bully Romance Fantasy Paranormal Shifters) - HEAT 4 out of 5

Enter the Wyvern All-Boys Academy as the Only Girl or Get Killed for Defying the Royal Decree

Diamonds and Dragons (Cruel Princes of Wyvern All-Boys Academy Book 1)

https://www.amazon.com/Diamonds-Dragons-Reverse-Fantasy-All-Boys-ebook/dp/B07SFV1PRH/

Roses and Emeralds (Cruel Princes of Wyvern All-Boys Academy Book 2)
https://www.amazon.com/Roses-Emeralds-Reverse-Fantasy-All-Boys-ebook/dp/B07TS1BKLT/

Silver and Starlight (Cruel Princes of Wyvern All-Boys Academy Book 3)
https://www.amazon.com/dp/B07VXVK2KV

Cruel Princes of Wyvern All-Boys Academy Complete Series Box Set
https://www.amazon.com/gp/product/B086V6ZJKH

BAD BOYS BILLIONAIRE BACHELORS CLUB (Standalone Novels)
Billionaire Romances – Heat 3 out of 5

Bidding on the Billionaire
https://www.amazon.com/gp/product/B07CB8VXFY

Baby Girl (Baby Girl #1)

Movie Merger
https://www.amazon.com/gp/product/B07BX7DZ4G

Buying the Billionaire
https://www.amazon.com/gp/product/B07BXC37RQ

Broken
https://www.amazon.com/gp/product/B07BX97343

Connect with Me!

Rachel Angel Newsletter (PNR) on Madmimi
http://madmimi.com/signups/5e9ebf668aa14b4890d8
affb0ce952f9/join

Rachel Angel Reader Group called Rachel Angel
Royal Readers
https://www.facebook.com/groups/881277658892159/

Rachel Angel Facebook Page
https://www.facebook.com/RachelAngelBooks/

Rachel Angel Bookbub
https://www.bookbub.com/authors/rachel-angel

Rachel's Amazon Author Page
https://www.amazon.com/Rachel-Angel/e/B00EHA11DO

Rachel Angel Goodreads Page
https://www.goodreads.com/author/show/7211708.Rachel
 Angel

Baby Girl (Baby Girl #1)

Rachel Angel Twitter
https://twitter.com/RachelRomances

Rachel Angel Instagram
https://www.instagram.com/rachelangelbooks/